**GROLIER
BOOK CLUB EDITION**

Based on WINNIE-THE-POOH, THE HOUSE AT POOH CORNER, WHEN WE WERE VERY YOUNG, and NOW WE ARE SIX, written by A.A. Milne and illustrated by E.H. Shepard and published by Elsevier-Dutton Publishing Co., Inc.

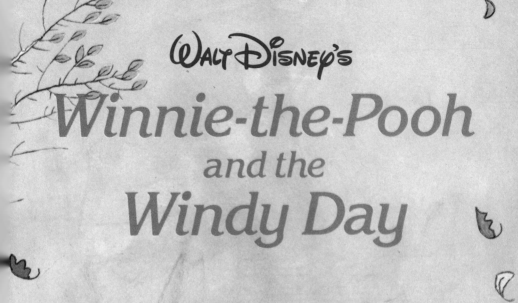

Walt Disney's
Winnie-the-Pooh
and the
Windy Day

First Pooh went to Piglet's house.
"Happy Windsday, Piglet," said Pooh.
"Hello, Pooh," squeaked Piglet.
Piglet was trying to sweep his yard.
But the wind blew the leaves everywhere.

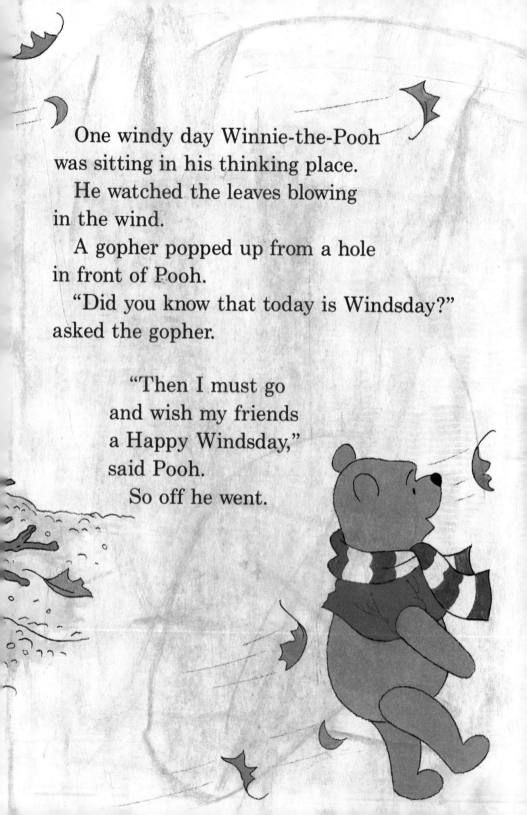

One windy day Winnie-the-Pooh
was sitting in his thinking place.
He watched the leaves blowing
in the wind.
A gopher popped up from a hole
in front of Pooh.
"Did you know that today is Windsday?"
asked the gopher.

"Then I must go
and wish my friends
a Happy Windsday,"
said Pooh.
So off he went.

Suddenly Piglet began to blow away too.
Pooh grabbed Piglet's sweater.
But the sweater began to unravel.
Soon Pooh was holding on to only a thread!

Piglet flew up,
up, up in the air.
    He pulled Pooh
behind him
on the ground.
    Along came
Kanga and her
baby, Roo.

    "Look, Mama!"
said Roo. "Piglet
is a kite!"
    Kanga waved
to Piglet.
    Piglet waved
back.

Pooh was pulled along faster and faster.

Eeyore the donkey was standing outside his new stick house.

Eeyore had just finished building it.

"There! Nothing will knock this down," Eeyore said proudly.

CRASH! The wind blew Pooh into the stick house.

"Well . . . nothing but Pooh," said Eeyore.

Rabbit was picking carrots
in his garden.

"My back hurts," Rabbit said.
"I wish someone would help me."
Just then the wind dragged Pooh
through the carrot patch.

Pooh's feet dug up
the carrots.

The carrots flew right
into the wheelbarrow.

"Happy Windsday!"
called Pooh.

Pooh and Piglet
sailed on to
Owl's house.

Inside Owl was trying to read.
But the strong wind shook
the tree.
Owl's tree house shook too.

Suddenly Owl heard
a thump on the window.
He turned around.
What a surprise!

"Hmm," said Owl,
"I did not know that
Piglet could fly."

Then Pooh
appeared at
the window
too.

Owl opened the window.
A gust of wind blew Pooh and Piglet in.
"Happy Windsday, Owl," said Pooh.

Pooh and Piglet flew across the room.
They landed in two chairs.
"How nice of you to drop in," said Owl.

Owl sat down with his friends.
The house swayed back and forth
in the wind.
A pot on the table slid over
to Pooh.

"Is there honey in this pot?"
asked Pooh.

"Yes, there is," said Owl.

"I love honey," said Pooh.

"Help yourself," Owl said.

The house swayed
some more.

The pot of honey slid
right into Pooh's arms.

Pooh lifted up the lid.

But suddenly the house tilted sharply.
The honey pot slid away from Pooh.
"Come back!" Pooh said.

The wind blew
harder and harder.
Owl's tree
leaned over . . .

. . . and crashed to the ground!
Owl's house fell to pieces.
The honey pot landed on Pooh's head.
Piglet landed on top of the honey pot.
"Piglet, are you hurt?" asked Owl.
"No," said Piglet.

"And are you
all right, Pooh?"
asked Owl.
"Yum . . . I mean
yes," said Pooh.

"But my house is not all right!"
said Owl.

"I AM sorry, Owl," Pooh said.

Along came Eeyore.

"Did Pooh crash into Owl's house too?"
asked Eeyore.

"It was the wind," said Pooh.

"Don't worry, Owl," said Eeyore.
"I will find you a new place to live."
And he slowly shuffled away.

The wind was still
blowing very hard.
  Then it began
to rain.
  "Let's go home,"
said Pooh. "I have
had enough of
Windsday."
  "So have I,"
said Piglet.

The windy day turned into a windy night.
And it rained and rained and rained.

The river overflowed.

The water came closer and closer to Piglet's door.

In the middle of the night Piglet woke up.

Piglet sat up in bed.

His bedroom was flooded!

His chairs and dresser were floating on top
of the water.

Even his bed bobbed up and down!

"Oh, oh," Piglet said. "What shall I do?"

Soon he had an idea.

Piglet climbed on a chair and floated
out the window.

Water was everywhere!
Piglet found a stick to use as an oar.
He steered his chair through the water.
"Hello! Hello!" called Piglet.
But there was no one around.

The rain fell
harder and harder . . .

. . . the wind blew
this way and that . . .

. . . and Piglet
was almost
blown overboard!

Pooh's house was flooded too.
"I must save my honey," said Pooh.
So he put his pots out on a branch.
"This is hard work," Pooh said.
"It's time for
a little honey."

Pooh began to
lick the honey.

Then he put his head
into the pot to lick
some more. . . .

His head got stuck . . .
and he fell off the branch!
"Help!" Pooh called.

Pooh fell into the river headfirst.

With his head in the pot, he floated
by Piglet.

"Pooh, oh Pooh!" Piglet called happily.

"I'm in here," said Pooh.

He sounded very sad.

Piglet pulled Pooh to safety.
But all of a sudden—
"Look out!" called Pooh.
"Help!" squeaked Piglet.
The two of them went over a waterfall!

The rain was stopping.

Christopher Robin went down to the riverbank to find his friends.

There was Owl riding on a log.

Rabbit, Tigger, Kanga, and Roo were safe in a tub.

"But where are Pooh and Piglet?" Christopher Robin asked.

No one knew!

Then Pooh came floating downstream.
"Hooray!" everyone cheered.
Pooh waved to his friends.
Piglet waved from the honey pot.

Christopher Robin
waded into the water and
rescued Pooh and Piglet.

"Pooh put me in
the honey pot to keep
me safe," said Piglet.
"Pooh, you are
a hero," Christopher
Robin said.

"Pooh saved Piglet," Christopher Robin
said. "We will have a hero party for him!"
Just then Eeyore walked slowly up
to the group.

"Good news," said Eeyore. "I have found an empty house. Owl can live there."

"That's wonderful!" said Christopher Robin. "Where is it, Eeyore?"

"Follow me," said Eeyore. He slowly shuffled away.

Eeyore led everyone up to a door.
"I've seen that door before," said Pooh.
"Pooh, that's MY house," whispered Piglet.

"It's Piglet's house!"
said Rabbit.

"So if Owl
moves in—"
said Kanga.
"—where
will Piglet
live?" asked
Roo.

"Piglet can live
with me," said Pooh.
"I'd like that,"
said Piglet.

Pooh gave Piglet a big bear hug.
"Piglet gave his house to a friend
without a home," said Christopher Robin.
"That makes Piglet a hero too. We will
have a two-hero party!"

The wind and rain had stopped.
Christopher Robin and his friends
set up a table on a dry hill.
And they all had a wonderful party!